GOD'S SMILE

COLLECTION OF SHORT STORIES

KUNNATHOOR RAJENDRAN

Contents

Acknowledgements   *vii*

Foreword   *ix*

1. The Cure   1

2. Hema   8

3. We Don't Want To Know...!   23

4. The Bride And The Bugs   31

5. Bhavayami   38

6. God's Smile   47

English Language

God's Smile- Collection of Short Stories

Author

Kunnathoor Rajendran

Rights Reserved

First Published March, 2022.

Publishers

Notion Press,
No.8, 3rd Cross St,
CIT Colony, Mylapore,
Chennai, Tamil Nadu 600004.
e-mail: publish@notionpress.com
online   bookstore: https://notionpress.com/read/
potpourri-1353520

Priced at: INR 149

Acknowledgements

Author's Note:

I scribbled these stories while on my 3rd assignment to Libya during 1994-1996. My Company then Unitech India, used to coordinate various events for the Indian Embassy, as its Regional Manager was the Chairman of Indian Community (ICA in general and IWA for women). The ICA used to publish an in-house magazine, the Ambassador of India being its patron editor. I remember that it used to remain in bundles in a corner of the Embassy reading room for public, and hardly anyone took much interest in it.

Once, while I was in the midst of supervising some administrative arrangement for some Indian event, a Bengali gentleman introduced me as the new editor of the magazine and asked me if I could contribute some writings to the magazine. I politely declined as I was sure that fictional writing is not my cup of tea. However he did not leave it there, but gently persisted till I wrote "Thy shall not return to Earth" which said about ghosts of two brothers who manages a lift from a Car driver and takes him to their repentant father etc., Surprisingly the story was received well and the editorial board was after me for regular contribution and my then RM Mr. Arora too felt that I should continue. Thus these stories followed, except perhaps HEMA, which I wrote in the last leg of my tenure. It was not a smooth affair. Some of the stories like, "We don't want to know", the Bug & God's smile etc., generated controversies, women readers in general, and the Ambassador stayed the publication of some issues, but people photocopied the available copies and were widely read. And these standoffs finally culminated to my early exit from Libya. Thereafter I mostly confided to my professional notes & reports, except perhaps a few articles in "Business Kerala" then run by Kalady Rice Millers Cluster Consortium. There too a satire on Secretariat bureaucracy had ensured its early folding up.

Adv Shri P.S. Sreedharan Pillai, the Hon'ble Governor of Goa, who read the manuscript was enthused and wanted to publish them through Vigil, Calicut that somehow remained on hold.

Thanks to MK Geetha, a journalist of standing, upon her initiative the stories are in print now, through the whole support of Shri Anand Krishnamurthy. At this point I warmly remember Shri Thomas, my colleague in Libya then who typed the scripts some 25 years back and encouraged me to write. I will not say that the characters, not all, are factionary etc., they indeed walked with me or crossed my paths.

May all rest in peace? Thank you so much for reading!

Author Biography:

Shri Kunnathoor Rajendran was born to K. P. Raghavan Pillai and K. Pankajaakshiyamma in 1947. He did his schooling in Koovapadi Ganapathivilasam High School and furthered his studies from Sree Sankara College, Kalady, Delhi University, Shree Venkitesara University and University of Sagar (M.A., M.Com, L.L.B.)

He served in Rural Electirification Corporation and Indian Road Construction Corporation. He was also an active participant of Delhi Malayalee Association. Wife: M. Kanakavalli, Children: R. Rajani, Mahendranath.

Address: Kanakam, Madampally, Cheraanalloor- 683544. Phone: 0484 2641933, Mobile: 9447190625. e-mail: kodanad@yahoo.com

Foreword

Of God(s), Ghost(s), Humans and...Animals!

'God's Smile', as the title of a short story collection in contemporary India might be slightly misleading-even with a smiling Buddha on the cover page! The Reader can't be faulted if s/he mistook it to be some spiritual anthology. Wait...it is not! Rather, it is an amazingly camouflaged mix of amusing tales blending the world(s) of humans, animals, ghosts and God(s)!

God's Smile is a collection of Six short stories- "The Cure", "Hema", "We don't want to know!", "The Bride and the Bugs", "Bhavayami", and the titular story. Each story transports us to varied yet engrossing locales. As we read through, we get to explore not only the world of humans, but also the animals-not only the mortal world, but also the immortals-and the God(s) play a part in both human and animal lives. Sometimes, just like in the *Animal Farm* (Orwell), Rajendran puts animals into an extended use as metaphors for human beings, and otherwise as (and in) contrast to human nature.

The anthology (and your reading process) begins with "The Cure". In fact, it is my personal favourite in this collection, as it throws light into the current politics in India. In the guise of a subtle story of a grandfather and his granddaughter, Rajendran subtly unveils a post-truth world in front of us. The opening line of the story "It is we who invented the Aeroplanes, and not those English, mind my girl, not those English", instantly reminds us of various popular (misleading) propagandas that we have come across from our ministers in the last decade or so.

Rajendran satirically mocks the (pseudo) theorists who claim of Plastic Surgery's origins in India with Lord Ganesha, Cow's urine to cure Cancer, Oxygen generation from Ducks, Nuclear Weapon as *Brahmastra* and so on. When Rajendran says the postmaster "came with names like Kudandan, Sudandan with anappropriate syllable fixed to the core word 'DANDAN' and when he ran out of Dandans he came upwith names like 'Karakan, Chorakan, Khorakan and the likes", we couldn't help bursting out in laughter; yet it ought to open our eyes too! The predicament of his granddaughter and his baby brother serves an eye opener to all of us.

"We don't want to know!" and "Bhavayami" are two stories that takes us through the lives (!!!) of ghosts! In the former, the setting happens to be a Banyan Tree, near the temple on the outskirts of the city, where ghosts meet and converse, where as in the latter, Rajendran blends the transitory and perpetual worlds, where bereaved son (Unni) converses with his father! "Bhavayami" takes to that ephemeral deep reality when father says- "In today's world when everyone is on the run after mirages, who has time to stop and listen to a muffled cry, a wailing heart, time to put a bowl of water to the cupped hands."

"God's Smile", the titular story, on the other hand, is a compelling take on the predicament and futility of animal lives at the hands of humans. Awaiting "to be cut and sliced and fried to be eaten by the masters who paid for us", two hens and a senior cock wail at the 'inhumane' (!!) slaughtering happening around them. As we read through, we start seeing metaphoric use of their actions, especially when the grand cock is said to possess a lot of clairvoyance power- "The grand cock peeped into their future and came with many remedies and suggestions and one such remedy was to eat some special stones with their grains. Notwithstanding his wisdom and clairvoyance powers the grand cock cannot contain his excitement when he had to deal with young hens and chics. For a closer scrutiny of their fate, he would bring them under his wings and if his wife was not watching, would give some quick rubs on their sensitive parts"- for sure, we are again transported to the human world and stories of several (fake) *bhabas* that we come across in our daily lives. Rajendran also brings in the authorial defence when the senior cock says "if he (the author) takes any name and bring a human being as a character he would be made to apologise both standing and stooping"!

"The Bride and the Bugs", juxtaposes the lives of bugs and humans, portraying the struggle for survival. Rajendran intertwines the desire for luxury and fame with the striking blow of fatality (or should I say futility?).

Of "Hema", I shall not speak much. Opening as a clichéd neighbourhood/childhood romance, it takes a lot of twists and turns to reach its climax. The portrayal of the titular heroine stands out, and so does Raghu's.

As I sum up, I must remark that Kunnathoor Rajendran's writing style would remind you of (if you are a Malayali) the ecriture of legends like Vaikkom Muhammed Basheer, Sanjayan, V.K.N. and so on. His satires are subtle yet profound, drawn from commonplace characters, and extremely touching and thought provoking. While reading through these stories, I also imagined them in Malayalam quite often; they would equally make a compelling read in the vernacular. I must also mention that endings of some of his stories contain what was design to O. Henry- the twist!

I honestly wish that this serves as a fruitful reading experience to all of you; I also wish that the author continues to write and publish more such thought-provoking tales!

Power to you!

Anand Krishnamurthy
Translator/Teacher/Columnist

Short Bio:

Anand Krishnamurthy is the Founder and Head of AK Creations AKademy, Cochin. He is currently a Ph.D. research scholar, under Dr. Latha Nair, in St,Teresa's College, Ernakulam. He is a regular columnist in the Grihashobha family magazine (titled *Aanandham*), under the Delhi Press Group. He edited an anthology of Indian Translations 'Potpourri: Poems and Tales from India', published by the Notion Press. He is also the recipient of "Teacher Stories Contest" organized by the Oxford University Press and SPELT. He was honoured with 'The Innovative Teacher Award' by the Rotary Club of Madras Coromandel in 2020. e-mail: anandkrishnamurthyak@gmail.com

ONE
THE CURE

The Cure

"It is we who invented the Aeroplanes, and not those English, mind my girl, not those English." The old man was excited and his words choked with emotion. Over them the aircraft was receding to the horizon and the roar of its engines became a humming. The old man and his grand daughter were walking around the park in front of their house. The park was in a state of neglect as the township management was always short of funds to maintain the park. Wild bushes and shrubs invaded the pathways, there were stagnated water pools, and the concrete benches provided were broken and invaded by moss. Yet the old man found that walking a few circles in the park in the morning, gave the much needed exercise for his otherwise stiff limbs. His grand daughter gave him company as her school was closed for vacation.

"Then who invented the aeroplanes grandfather", asked the girl. "It is our Rishis & Munis, my girl Our Rishis & Munis" the old man was thrilled.

"Who were they?" The girl asked.

"They were great saints who lived in deep forests, always meditating", the old man explained.

"If they lived in deep forest always meditating, why did they require an aeroplane", the girl was getting curious.

"Oh" the old man fumbled for an answer. "They might have required them to visit their friends or they might have made them for the kings." The old man continued his explanation. "Dont you know that Ravana had abducted Sita in one such aeroplane and Lord Rama travelled in that aeroplane on his journey back to Ayodhya."

"I am sure Sita would not have liked it", said the girl. What? "Travelling in Ravana's aeroplane", the girl was in a doubt.

"No, no she was travelling with her husband and Ravana had been killed", the old man dispelled the girl's doubt.

The girl kept quiet. For some reason she could not appreciate that Sita had to travel in her abductor's conveyance.

"Did you ever travel in an aeroplane, grandpa", the girl queried.

"Yes, yes, many times", told the old man which was a lie. He was a postmaster in the post office at his village and his only connection with anything related to aeroplanes was the post marking of airmail envelopes which came to families from persons working in Gulf countries.

After his retirement he found life getting harder. It was not due to any economical reasons, he had enough income from agriculture. His pension money was enough to take care of his personal needs. His son-in-law was in Dubai and his daughter lived in the nearby town for the sake of Public School education for the children. He had a son in Delhi who also occassionally sent money to the parents. So money was never the problem. The problem was that his wife was hard of hearing and she made him run around on petty errands. To make her understand what he has done or not done he had to keep his pitch always high and that made him nervous. His only solace was the company of his friends who regularly met under the banyan tree near the temple. There he was more a listener than a speaker.

Things then changed unexpectedly. One day after collecting his pension he was coming to his daughter's house. Some public meeting was going on in the park in front of her house. The orator was describing at length what a glorious past the country had and how the English people appropriated the great inventions of the Rishis and Munis of India. The orator represented some communal outfit which had its headquarters somewhere in North-India and he was in an election campaign on behalf of a political party which had made the revival of Hinduism as their election plank. The postmaster was so impressed by what he heard and was thrilled to see that he got a ready audience among his group when he reproduced some of the wisdom he picked from the orator in the park. The postmaster enjoyed his new role and started crediting more and more inventions to Rishis and Munis whose name none had heard ever. He came with names like Kudandan, Sudandan with anappropriate syllable fixed to the core word 'DANDAN' and when he ran out of Dandans he came upwith names like 'Karakan, Chorakan, Khorakan and the likes. In the beginning he credited bombs, missiles, nuclear warhead, aeroplanes, rockets to these saints and later put typewriters, bicycle, sewing machine, table fan etc., also on account of these Rishis who existed in his fertile imagination only. When he ran out of mechanical contraptions he turned to medicines.

"See, my little girl", the old man pointed out to the wild bushes and shrubs in the park. Our Rishis used to make life saving and preserving medicines from these plants. They had a cure for any disease, be it cancer, Aids, TB, cold and what not. They could do surgery as well, may be better than our present day doctors.

The girl looked at the old man with awe, "Was it so Grandfather", she asked.

"Why not, when Lakshman and his monkey army was annihilated by Meghanath, the son of Ravana, did not Hanuman bring them back to life by bringing a medicinal plant from our place. In fact, he brought the whole mountain when he had a problem of identifying the right plant", the old man explained.

"How did he know which plant cures which disease grandfather", was the child inquisitive.

"That our Rishis had it all written in books which the English took away from our country and now they make those medicines as allopathy", the old man was getting angry.

"Did the Rishis know English otherwise how did the English people understand what was written in those books", the child was innocent.

"No, no, they were written in Sanskrit and these English people learnt Sanskrit to understand what was written by the Rishis", the old man clarified.

"I tell you my child, only our government sends its army to those English countries and gets back our valuable books written by our Rishis, our country can progress, otherwise all our work is nonsense", he spoke in anger. The old man was furious, in fact, he was in the midst of a signature campaign in his village for a memorandum to be sent to the President, urging him to send the Indian army to all

European capitals to get back the books and drawings or whatever the English might have taken from India on science and medicine. But his daughter called him to town as her son had fallen sick and needed constant medical care.

They were walking back to home. Both were silent. The child was remorseful. Her brother was sick for the last two weeks, he was gripped by some fever and the doctor was attending to him at home. The grandfather had come to escort the doctor to home and back and also to get medicine and other items for the house as her mother had to remain in the house always to look after the boy.

"Will there not be medicine in those bushes for Kannan, grandfather", the girl asked the old man.

"May be, but who knows, the English had taken away all our knowledge", the old man replied in disgust.

The girl was thoughtful, if only the English had left those valuable information, Kannan need not to have remain in bed for all these days. Three years old Kannan, her brother was her sole company. It was to him she used to narrate the happenings in the school, who whether understood or not was an encouraging listener and made appropriate noises while listening to her sister. She used to pillion ride him in her tricycle brought by her father from Dubai. Now he has been ill since two weeks and she was always lonely with none to play with or speak to.

She went to Kannan who was sleeping. She touched him, his body was hot. She felt so sad, if only she know the right plant as known by the Rishis, she could have cured him. As the grandfather had told her, the medicines are made by crushing the leaves and seeds or sometimes the roots. Unfortunately, she did not know which plant it could be that could have the miraculous power to cure her Kannan, so that he could play with her as before. After her bath and breakfast she went to the Pooja room in the house and stood before the picture of Lord Krishna. In the picture, the Lord was holding his flute and was standing beneath a tree. The girl looked closer, Oh Krishna, please tell me which is that plant in the park that can Cure the fever of Kannan. Oh Krishna, please tell me, please. Then an idea occured to her. In the backdrop of Lord Krishna in the picture, there were some plants with flowers. It could be one of those plants otherwise how could they come in the picture of Lord Krishna. She looked still closer and could identify some plants that she had seen in the park.

She was greatly relieved. Now she knew everything. She knew the cure. Her mother in the drawing room was talking to a visitor who had come to enquire about Kannan. The old man had left for the market. She went back to the park and looked among the wild bushes. After considerable search, she located a plant which to her young mind was almost like the one in the picture of Lord Krishna. She carefully pulled it out from the earth, rolled it in a piece of paper lying in the park and stealthly got back home without being noticed by her 'mother who was still talking to the visitor. She went to the bathroom, crushed the whole plant with the help of a stone. The plant and the juice did give a burning sensation in her eyes. She carefully poured the liquid in a glass tumbler and tip-toed back to Kannan.

The boy was still in sleep. She went near him. Oh Kanna, Kanna, she called him mildly, jerking his body. He opened his eyes and looked at her blankly. In a low tone she said, "Look Kanna, this is the medicine from our Rishis, you will be cured in a minute. The English were not allowing us to know the medicine, but I understood it from Lord Krishna, be a good boy and drink this, you will be alright and we will go for cycling thereafter".

On recognising his sister, the boy tried to smile. She slowly poured the liquid to his mouth. He was jerking his head. She pressed his cheeks and poured the whole liquid through the open mouth. The child swallowed some and spit out some. She held his mouth, so that his cries were not heard. The boy jerked his head a few more times and remained quiet thereafter. His eyes were closed. The girl was happy, he is getting cured. She touched his body. Slowly the temperature was coming down. She was overwhelmed with joy. "Oh, my Rishis and Munis what a wonder cure you were knowing, Oh Lord Krishna, you showed me the right plant" her joy was beyond bounds.

She ran to her mother, she could not control herself, "I have cured Kannan, mother I have cured Kannan, by the medicine of our great Rishis & Munis, what if the English did not tell us what medicine they took from India, Lord Krishna showed me the right plant, Kannan is alright now, he is alright." Her mother was perplexed, she could not make out much, she ran towards the room where the boy was sleeping.

The girl ran out of the house to look for the cycle. She heard the shrieking of her mother from inside, sometimes she is like that, she will find about it afterwards, now first the cycle...

TWO
HEMA

Hema

"Then what happened" the S.P. was showing his annoyance.

"Hold me" Hema said, He resumed his confession.

She extended her hands to me. The rocks were slippery. The river was gushing past through the rocks. We were on the ridge across the river. The legend was that the Demons attempted to erect a barrage across the river before dawn, but had to abandon the task midway when some mischievous cock announced the arrival of dawn much ahead of the time. The barrage, in course of time, became a ridge leaving a large gap at the centre through which the water gushed, down to the rocks below. Only dare-devils could venture to walk through the slippery rocks upto the point of water fall.

And Hema was a dare-devil, always. She was elder to me by about 2 years and always took it as her natural right to command me. I was one class junior to Hema in the school. My mother was a maid at Hema's house. In some distant way my mother was related to Hema's father and when we lost our father, no sir, he did not die, he just abandoned our mother and went to Tamil Nadu where he is said to have had another family. In every respect, a brother, a sister, youngest us of all, were dependent on the good will of Hema's parents and that good will they had in plenty.

Hema's father had some shop in Singapore and he used to come home once a year. Upto her V^{th} standard Hema too was in Singapore and then she and her mother came home to settle for good. Hema's mother and an uncle looked after the rubber plantations, rice fields etc., assisted by a supervisor sort of a person.

Hema had an elegance. She was fair complexioned and had all the ingredients to be termed a beauty, but it was her elegance that attracted me to her. It was my duty to escort her to school and back. She always talked to me in commanding tone loaded with arrogance. I enjoyed it. I faithfully carried her school bag, umbrella, water bottle etc. on the way to school and back and she seldom kept company with other girls. My friends in the class used to make fun of me for being her escort. Hema knew it too, but she never appeared to have taken note of it and made me carry her belongings to and from school. As I told you Sir, I did like it, No, I never felt I was doing a menial job. Instead I felt that I was serving a queen and it was upon me, not only to carry her books and tiffin carrier but also to protect her from invisible enemies who, I always dreamed, would come galloping through the fields, we used to pass on the way to school.

Yes, yes I was a dreamer all along. What all I dreamt. I might have been twelve and she thirteen. While returning from school I used to walk with her in tandem. It was an enchanting sight to see the rays of the evening sun glowing upon the rear of her neck. She always plaited her hair in two bands. The rear of her neck and the back visible through the low cut blouse all glowing with rays of the setting sun, as if so many marigolds were in bloom, to watch that, was an ecstasy for me. I can remember it even now Sir, So many so many marigolds, Sir.

Then one day she did not come to school. I waited for her and when she did not show up, I went to my mother who was in Hema's house. I was told that she is indisposed. I came away sullen. I felt that the distance to and from school had increased manifold and I was desolate, to walk without the belongings Hema, I felt myself useless. I did not talk much either at home or at school. I was longing for the return of Hema.

She showed up on the fourth day. There was this change. She was glowing. A transformation which remained abstract to me. I could not control my excitement. I asked "why you did not come to the school these four days" "I was not well" she was curt and handed over to me her books and tiffin carrier.

"What was wrong with you, tell me, tell me", I pestered her. We are standing in front to her house.

She called my mother. "Tell you son not to pester me. " She said rudely. The slap came unexpectedly- "you imprudent, behave yourself". My mother was angry beyond description.

Hema laughed on my shame. She laughed all through the way to school. I learnt about the reason for her absence from my friends. They explained it as repulsively as they could.

Four years rolled away just like that. After passing the Xth Standard, Hema joined the women's college about 40 Km. away from our village. I do not know how I was able to withstand her parting. The solace was that she used to come home once a month to stay for two or three days. I knew the timing of the bus. Yet at least one hour ahead I used to arrive at the bus stop. To me, since joining the college, she had mellowed and started behaving in a friendly manner with me. She used to talk to me about the college, the teachers, her new friends and so on. I used to listen attentively without missing a word. Her friends also had become my friends, though I never saw them. And I would enquire about them by name. To me, to be near Hema and to hear her, were the ultimate bliss. She used to enquire about my studies and to impress her, I did well in the class, and came with highest marks always.

Behind my house there is a river. The other bank of the river are lined with Teak Plantations. Teak plantations lead to forest, which is about 5 k.m. up. Where the Teak Plantations ended and forests started there was a rock formation, something like a big tennis court. This at the easter-side had a cave like structure. A freak by nature. It was quite big and something like a shrine with an ante chamber. People took shelter under this structure when the rains caught them unexpected and the tribals at times cooked their hunt there. There was small stream running at the western side and the stream had flower bearing trees on either side of its course. I used to walk upto this place occasionally. Sit there hours together day dreaming, that this is my place, where Hema is my queen and our subjects are scattered over the forest. Once in those caves I could always feel her presence, I could hear the clattering of her anklets. Once I did tell her about her abode which I had discovered for her. As usual she kept a stiff upper lip and looked at me tauntingly.

Since joining the college, she used to wear a half sari too over her long skirt and blouse. I would walk behind her carefully putting my feet over her foot prints and the very thought that my feet were touching the same sand which was touched by her feet, was electrifying to me. And some times I would stand over her foot prints for minutes together. Once she asked me what I had been doing standing attention. I stuttered for an answer, but finally managed to tell her the truth in broken sentences. She did not laugh. She just smiled. I felt relieved. I was expecting an angry outburst. She let me off, that is how I thought about it.

After passing Xth Standard I joined an Institute newly started near our school to teach typewriters and shorthand. That was the only higher education my mother could afford for me. I studied for one year and by that time Hema had done her pre-degree course and was at home. I used to dutifully call on her whenever I could get time and offer myself for any services to her however trivial it could be. My mother was planning to send me to Calcutta where some cousin of hers was reportedly in good position, to put up me on a job. She was preparing for my departure and journey.

One day I found a few strangers alighting from a car in front of Hema's house. I knew that Hema was at home but had no clue as to why those strangers had come. Among them, one stuck of my notice; He had sharp features and there was viciousness in his looks which I could neither decipher nor explain. He was in his thirties.

That night I asked my mother who those people were had come to Hema's house.

"They had come to see Hema" Mother said; She also told that the man who was seeking Hema was around thirty and has some business in Banglore. I sat dumbfounded. I did not utter a word. I ate a little. An unexplainable gloom had descended upon me. I passed a sleepless night.

"Are you sketching a story for rendering a confession" The S.P. was getting angry. May be he was getting late for the club.

Sorry sir, But I must explain to you all the details, mustn't I? He submitted. "Go on, go on", The" S.P. was getting impatient. He resumed his confession. By that time we had moved to a small house adjacent to Hema's. The house was built by liberal helping by Hema's father. I met Hema the next day.

"Yesterday some people had to come to see you I am told" I stuttered. "So does that make any difference to you" She appears displeased with my query. I had no answer

"Why don't you speak up what is in your clumsy head" she was getting furious. "I don't want you to marry that man", I had suddenly gained courage.

"Nor do I, I did not like too. He appears to be too crude for me. Then what option have I. Mother and uncles have felt that he is the best choice for me. Had my father been here I could have persuaded him to drop this alliance. It will be too late, if at all he arrives for the marriage". Hema was unbelievably dejected over the happenings that were taking over her.

I wanted to say that I wanted her to come with me and that we could go to Delhi or Bombay and I would look after her like a queen etc., etc., but I knew that these were only my wishes and I was the proverbial beggar riding over them.

I knew that I would not do that. If at all I did that, my whole family would have been thrown to the streets by Hema's uncles and others. And then Hema was accustomed to a certain standard of living which I would never even hope for. My helplessness started enveloping me; I felt, Hema, We, all were in a different world; I heard so many conch shells wringing in my ears. Amidst that I heared Hema saying "Some time I feel why can't both of us go away somewhere, After a pause she continued, "I know its not possible, you are a clumsy dreamer", She walked away.

That night I left my village, It was a long journey, Doing all sorts of menial jobs I found my way to Delhi. I moved from one petty job to another. I was matriculate and knew typing. Finally I landed myself as a sales clerk. It was almost two years after I had left home. I joined the evening classes, took my first degree at the fifth year after I left home, By that time my job also steadied. used to send whatever money I could to home. My younger brother joined a polytechnic, the sister who was the youngest, was in high school. After five years I returned home there were notable changes in my house. It was fairly modified, my mother was not going for menial jobs in Hema's house but she was to visit them once a day. When partition took place at my father's house, his brothers gave part of his share to us, with which my mother bought a small piece of ice field.

Of course, I enquired with my mother about Hema. She was at Bangalore I was told and all was not well with her. Though five years had passed after her marriage, she had no children. Hema's father was back home for good: There had been some dispute over the properties between Hema's father and her uncles. From the disjointed soliloquy of my mother I could guess that there was something seriously wrong with Hema's marriage. "They are big people and rich, why should we bother what happens or not happens with them" mother dismissed the whole topic.

I thought of going to Banglore to see her, but I was apprehensive of what sort of reception I might get from her or her husband. I went back to Delhi. Another two years passed and I took a diploma in management and found myself as a Jr. Executive in a fairly well established company.

I engrossed myself with my job, night classes, correspondence courses, all in fact to keep myself occupied so that I would not keep thinking about Hema. In a way.it was an escapism.

But the fact was that I had no escape, right from the night I left my village, Hema was with me, invisible but alive in my thoughts, dreams and in the very air I breathed. I built a make believe world around her. In my fantasies she was my queen to be served, not to be possessed. In my world of dream, we travelled through highways and hill tracks, in every conceivable form of transport. We visited temples together, rowed boots, went for mountaineering, trecking, thats all, not beyond. I always thought that should not fail her. To get her appreciation I did every job well and moved higher in the corporate ladder. I conversed with Hema each night, told her what I did that day, and what I might do the next day. I seldom went to my native place. I was afraid I might confront Hema and then my dreams would break. In my dreams she was as I saw her last, that is before leaving my village. I was content that she was with me everywhere. She in my thought, was my motivation

I come across Meera, then a practising lawyer attached to the legal firm that was handling our company cases. I was involved in a case with one of our clients. At the very first sight the similarity of Meera to Hema struck me. Meera had the identical dimples of Hema. Meera also belonged to a Nair family not very far from my native place. Her father was an undersecretary in Delhi, since retired, He was looking for an acceptable groom who would carry her off so that he can move to his native place. Everything began to fit perfectly and Meera became Meera Nair soon. We were married at the Avyappa temple in Delhi.

To me Meera was a medium, yes a live medium for Hema. I found out that I could transform Meera to Hema, any time 1 felt so. She was my medium to reach Hema. Fine. Meera did notice that I had some behavioral abnormalities. But she did not bother. Her interest was more in her profession. And we both felt happy the way it worked out. Our first and only daughter was born in the second year of our marriage.

Yes sir, yes sir, I know that I had come to make a confession, not to present fiction and I cannot invent stories. All through my life I have been in the world of businesses of others. I am sure Sir, you will appreciate these details when I finish the narration as to how, Hema was done away from this word and unless I am saying it all in detail, you cannot make a full proof case that would withstand the onslaught of the prosecution. So please bear with me Sir. I am coming closer to the end of my narration. As I told you Sir, I was avoiding meeting Hema. Last week I had been to Banglore, in connection with a conference on sales promotion of our products. Normally I avoided going to Bangalore as I always apprehended that I would come across with Hema and my make believe world would collapse. Then I was the choice of the M.D. to attend the conference and I was sounded to be incharge Karnataka - Madras region. So I went. I was put up in a Hotel in the contonment area. Yes, a Five-Star Hotel. See how from a table. Cleaning lad to an occupier in one of the best rooms in a five star hotel. On the second day of my arrival I was standing in the balcony. Rays of the evening sun were grazing on me. I thought that the same sun rays might be grazing over Hema too. I was breathing the same air, standing under the same sky I felt an urge that I should see

Hema. I telephoned to the reception for a car. I had a vague idea of the location of Hema's house.

From the telephone directory I picked up her husband's name and with the telephone number there was the brief address. It was not very difficult to locate the house once I entered that aristocratic housing vihar. It was very simple, Sir, the poor people's dwelling units would be named colony or nagar and the richmen's 'Vihar's'. Her house in one of those Vihars'.

With trepedation I pressed the calling bell, and waited. I started sweating. My mouth began to go dry. I felt my palpitation rising. And slowly the front door opened and there was Hema. She was more plum and radiated a glow which I only could see. She did not show any excitement on seeing me nor did I expect any.

"Come" she said matter of factly.

I followed her to drawing room.

"I was passing this way, I thought I should call on you" I stuttered.

"What for? Why can not you say that you have come to see me". I gulped. "Where is your wife?" She asked.

We sat without speaking a word. Time ticked away.

"I will bring tea for you" said Hema.

"No, No," I attempted to protest.

"Doesn't matter She said and went to the interior of the house.

I started looking at various showpieces in the drawing room. The show case contained many artifacts and I moved closer to have a better look.

"What are you doing there and who are you? The questions came in rapid fire. I turned around. There he was. Hema's husband. May be, lost in thoughts I did not hear his car coming

"How are you" I moved closer to him extending my hand.

"That's OK, tell me who you are and what you are doing here."

He was least hospitable.

"I am Raghu, from Hema's place. We used to go the school together" I fumbled with my answer.

"So it is you, who used to tail her to school and back and still keep writing to her all those letters." He was becoming menacing.

"No, No" I attempted to protest, but my sound was not audible even to me.

"Leave him alone" Hema was back with coffee.

"Oh, you are ready for reception of your ex-school lover".

He laughed mockingly, and shouted unexpectedly "You, you, bastard sweep off from this place"

I stood stupefied. I did not, rather I could not move myself. He started pushing me to the door by my neck. I stayed put. Hema tried to pull him back, saying "Please, for Gods sake, leave him alone, he will go, don't hurt him, please". Then he turned toward her and started slapping her. The blows were falling on her face, her neck, her cheeks, on the blooming marigold fields: That was the last straw, I picked up the engraved dagger from the show-case and before Hema could complete. NO, stuck the dagger right through his back. That was it, he sank like a sack. Hema stood blinking, colour draining from her cheeks, she was also sinking, I caught hold of her.

"Run" I said, "Run Hema, run" I began dragging her. I closed the front door, then the gate. She followed me as in a trance. I hailed a taxi. Once in the Hotel I booked two seats for Cochin in the first available flight.

In the air-craft Hema came out of her stupover. "Why did you do it and what we will do now, The Police, My God, the Police will catch-up I am sure. Oh my God she started sobbing soundlessly.

"Dont you worry", I said "None will know it in another 2-3 days. By that time we will be in our rock palace. None could reach there. You know the place" I tried to assure her. She did not say anything. She appeared to be normal thereafter. In the Taxi she answered me id monosyllables and kept looking at the landscapes that were rushing by.

At last the taxi reached the church, from where one had to walk to reach my rock palace. But to my surprise, I found a fair road is going through the plantations. "Take that road" I told the driver. Trucks and Jeeps were crossing us and some time were overtaking us.

"Stop, Stop" I cried. The car had reached the place where once my rock palace stood, now where are those rocks, where is my cave? my mouth went dry. There was nothing. A huge stone quarry stood where my palace had been. All blasted, the rock formations, the caves, the court yard everything. I stood there gazing. I could not face her. Tears started rolling down in my face.

"Pay the car driver" said Hema. The' taxi was waiting. I pulled out my purse. I did not count. From the broad smile of the driver I could make out that he got more than he hoped. I stood rooted at the site of my vanished palace. Don't be disheartened "Hema was by my side. You did the best and what could be for me. It is all fated this way. She started stroking my hair. Dark clouds were accumulating over the mountain top.

I heard the thunder and saw flashes of lightening that preceded them. The rain came roaring. It slashed us wet to the core. I could see that Hema had regained her usual self and she seemed least perturbed by what happened at her residence, a few hours before, may be days before.

"Let us walk", she said, I followed. We walked through the rain. A Small path took us up and upto the up stream of the river. The dried leaves soaked in water made squeezing sounds on our foot-steps. We trecked on and we reached the barrage which the Demons had built. Water was roaring down through the gap in the barrage. There were no human beings around. The mountain loomed large over the reservoir. We stood in silence. I stared at her, I could not believe myself. Hema, too near to me, with in my reach.

Drenched by the rain completely. Her body curves, transparent through the white saree that wrapped her. Then un-expectedly she said "Raghu, we must walk over these boulders and should feel the water fall. "No, No, I protested, it is dangerous, No we should go back

Hema did not bother to listen to me. She started climbing over the boulders, I followed.

"Hold me", She extended her hand. The boulders were slippery. We slipped but never fell. Crawling inch by inch we reached the boulder at the beginning of the gap through which the water was gushing down, splashing over the boulder. The splashed water formed a mist. Hema was so thrilled. She bent over and dipped her hand through the gushing water.

"Stop that Hema, stop that, you will fall down", I was in tears by shouting. You are scared are you not, scared, scared like very time. You could have come with me, before my marriage, but you were scared.

You are a coward, a coward, a clumsy dreamer, a dreamer that is all. Then you killed my husband, you are a murder a murder Ho, HO. She laughed hysterically. An unknown rage slowly began to take over me. My fear was receding. I balanced myself on the rock. Held her by armpit and slapped with full force. She was stunned by my unexpected violence. I began swinging my hand and my blows fell over her. The wasted adornment, the humiliation all came rushing to my mind. I might be mad. I kept swishing my hand. But Hema was not there. I shuddered. Where is my Hema? I cried "Hema, Hema." All this may be a dream and should be a dream. I pinched myself, I was senseless. I started crawling back over the boulders to the shore.

Once on the shore I started running down-stream, shouting all the time Hema, Hema. I spotted a white object floating in the middle of the river. Could it be Hema? I tried to keep track of the object but I could not. I lost my Hema for ever, the river took her for ever. I have nowcome to you to confess, all that I have done and that I have caused Hema's death and killed her husband too.

The SP began to tap on his desk. He picked up the receiver and dialled a number. "I think you can come" said he.

That narrator was not caring. He seemed to be lost in his thought but at the same time appeared to be relived of a great burden he seemed to be carrying.

"Have some coffee" offered the SP, and he signalled to a constable who was within earshot.

The lady and the doctor entered together. The lady walked upto the narrator and held his head to her bosom and started stroking his hair. He wept like a child and she pressed him closer to her.

Holding him as close to her as she could and slowly she lead him out of the room.

"What did he say", asked the doctor.

"It is all in those tapes, the SP pointed towards a tape recorder and the winding spool

"Thank you so much, Thank you", said the doctor.

That is OK you had already told me of this therapy of his, but what exactly is his problem, he was so convincing and brilliant" wondered the SP.

It is something like Erotomania, with a running streak of Paranoia", He lives in a make believe world, a world full of his delusions and illusions. For the last two years he is under my care. He is improving and this asking for a confession etc., is in the process of his recovery". Explained the doctor.

His wife, a lawyer" queried the SP

"No, No, she is house wife much devoted and attached to him" said the doctor.

"Who is this Hema? any idea?, The S.P. was getting curious.

OH, she, I think a girl of his neighbourhood, who was married to somebody in Bangalore. It seems this fellow had a fixation over her which was dormant all these years. About two years ago she was reportedly killed by her husband and since then this now fellow has been out of his fulcrum. Excuse me, let me join them, shall see you in the club" the doctor hurried out.

S.P. come to his seat. He dialled the intercom and said in the mouth piece "Check what this ..... Erotomania means" and send in that Baba who had been duping people telling the where their moles lies, and not where there fortune. He is due for a good thrashing"

The S.P readied himself.

THREE

WE DON'T WANT TO KNOW...!

We don't want to know...!

Ghost Nair met his Liberator Ghost Kurup when both were floating towards the usual meeting place of Ghosts, A Banyan Tree, near the temple on the outskirts of the city.

As usual Ghost Nair extended all courtesies to his Liberator, now Ghost Kurup, who on that day appeared to be a little uneasy.

In the world of the dead like Nair & Kurup a Liberator is one who liberates or causes to liberate the soul from the confines of one's physical body. t is common knowledge that every human being has to have a soul which shall remain confined to a body and shall experience and witness all sorrow, pleasure, enlightenment, and all that is transacted through the sensory organs of the body. As the pleasure comes more by evil or devil the sorrow has to catch up to bring such experiences to an equilibrium and the sorrow which normally outweighs pleasure has to be inflicted through the body, and the body becomes a miserable jail, for the soul, which though not much of its choice, has to undergo all the humiliations and sufferings not originally intended to by the Creator. Once liberated from the confines of the body, the soul becomes free and floatable like U S Dollars and every soul look for such a liberator.

In the mortal world such an act of liberation is referred to as MURDER and the Liberator as MURDERER and we all knew that he shall be the object of contempt and hatred and at times get liberated by the State through due procedure of law, if not already lynched by the survivors of his victim.

In the world of humans Nair was Headmaster of a local school where Kurup's wife Nalini was the music teacher. Kurup was a rustic farmer having paddy fields, coconut groves, orchards and a rice-mill too. Because Kurup had to be busy with mundane things like supervising the ploughing, harvesting, running the rice-mil, plucking the coffee seeds, nursing the orchards etc. thereby having little time to be romantic with his wife, who had a taste for finer things of life and what Kurup was doing had the least priority in her scheme of dreams. Nair was too willing and glad to fill this void, and for everyone it was a happy going till one day Kurup happened to be at the School around 12.00 noon just to see why his wife had not reached home, though the day was abruptly declared Holiday due to the passing away of a great soul, A former Prime Minister, who was in the chair for six months only before being pulled down by his own people. The school had only two closed rooms, one for the Headmaster which housed the School office as well and the other a store where the items of games and sundry were kept. The class rooms were open from either side, Nalini attended the office jobs too during leisure periods, a convenient alibi deviced by Nair for them to be together whenever possible.

Having not found his wife in the office room which had the doors ajar, Kurup proceeded to the store room at the other end of the school building from where some hustling sounds were coming. The door was closed from inside, so Kurup peeped through the slightly parted window and what he could see was neither pleasing nor tolerable to him though it was extremely pleasing to both Nair and Nalini in the posture they were. Kurup forced entered into the store and liberated both Nair and his own wife with an iron spike that came handy.

Later, after due procedure of Law, Kurup was liberated by the order of a Session's Judge who tried him for murder (in the mortal world). He lost in appeal too. In the transit world of dead both Nair and Nalini heartily welcomed their Liberator. Once free from the physical body feeling of jealousy, possessiveness, hatred etc. had no place and now all of them Nair, Kurup and Nalini float together in their Ghost status. Nalini floats with either of them as she pleases and nobody cares.

Now a legitimate question arises, if there is nobody having deprived of the same in the mortal world how one gauges the feelings of the other. It is very simple. It is just like blotting. One becomes the blotting paper for the others feelings. Thus in the transitory world of dead where our Kurup, Nair and others are withering away their balance time, each is aware of the exact thoughts of the other and each can visualise the other in any shape and form they prefer to.

This is not only in respect of those in their world but also in respect of the mortal world where they can see but cannot be seen and can hear but cannot be heard. They are all in this transitory stage because they were liberated from their physical bodies prematurely.

Each body assigned to a soul has to run a full course and the soul has to wait till the body ages and becomes ripe for heavenly abode when all the body system will fail and shall surrender its function, then the soul having been freed from a body that has run its full term will go for the ultimate Union, in which case it need not and does not transit through the world or state through which our Ghost Nair & Kurups are passing. But when the death is pre-imposed by an act of liberation whether by murder or by an accident, the soul has to wait till drawn to the ultimate UNION for which they wait infinitely. During this waiting period, they can be wherever they wish to be, hearing and seeing what their survivors think of them often to their utter agony and discomfort. The tragedy is that they have no escape too. Time has no meaning to them. Like in a swing they go back and forth of time. One can swing back to generations that preceded him and forth to generations that will follow him. Then you can, unlike the swing we fasten on tree branches, position the swing at any angle from its fulcrum. So you can float with your forefathers like a fish swimming upstreams, or you can float with the generations that are waiting for their destined part in the mortal world. It is all upto you to decide where you want to position your swing.

Mostly by compulsion of habit that could not be totally left behind in the mortal world, Nair did enquire with Kurup the cause of his uneasiness as Nair could blott the mental state of Kurup:

You knew, my Nair, said Kurup, "since I was liberated by that Sessions Judge order, my son and daughter are alone. My brother and his family have moved into my house. He is syphoning what he can, out of the income but cannot own my properties as they will devolve upon my children once they attain maturity under the Law. Therefore he and his wife were, for some time, trying to get my children out of their way. They are afraid of liquidating them as they will be caught by the watchful eyes of my wife's relatives who are keeping a strict vigil over the happenings at my home.

"Then what did he do?" queried Nair.

Oh! he has now arranged my daughter to be kidnapped and sold to some brothel agent in Bombay.

"How bad", sympathaised Nair.

"Not that bad'", continued Kurup peeped a bit ahead like I peeped through that school window', Nair blushed at the reference of the Store room.

"What did you see", Nair was curious.

My brother has planned the kidnapping on the day of the annual festival of our local temple. But that day the caparisoned elephant with diety mounted on it will run berserk by a mischief of my son. In the stampede that will follow my brother will be crushed and shall soon join us. His wife will have a dislocated pelvis and shall be bed-ridden for life. But she will join my brother here in a couple of years from now and by that time my children will be majors and my daughter will be happily wedded to the nephew of my wife and my son will look after his share of property better than me.

Then why worry? quipped Nair.

"See Nair", reasoned Ghost Kurup," I knew that once out of that stupid world of mortals we and they have no relation and we are strangers, yet that, total obliviousness comes only after we are taken into the Great Union, because by compulsion we move amidst our kith and kin and their both well-being and ill-being haunt us. See our helplessness in that, we knew what is in store for them but cannot warn them. The feelings that were once so strong and formed the basis of our existence out there have no meaning here, yet we are not totally free from them too. All these slated happenings have put me off", explained Kurup.

The rest of the distance to the Banyan tree they floated in silence. When they reached the meeting place, it was full of other Ghosts and each had a story to tell what they knew about time ahead and happenings that await each of their kith and kin whom they have left behind in the mortal world.

Aunt Rugmani knew that her newly married daughter who has gone to join her husband in Gujarat will be set on fire for insufficient dowry. Ghost Verghese who floated to Delhi and back to see his son knew the boy will that marry a local girl and will stop sending money to his ailing mother back in Kerala. There ought to be pleasant happenings too but at the end they are out-numbered by the miserable happenings and every one knew that in the Kaliyug for the mortal world it has to be so. Yet they were highly sad of their knowledge.

"Oh LORD! save us from this agony of knowing what is awaiting for all those we have left behind", lamented a Ghost who came to the transit world much early.

"Think of those times, how anxious we were to know the future and how much money and time we wasted lining up before astrologers and soothsayers to have a glimpse of what is in store for us", sighed another "Yes, yes, agreed another. My wife used to be at Krishnaji's residence on every Friday sharp at 6.00 a.m. to hear about her future fortune.

"Who Krishnaji?", exclaimed one.

The gentleman from Andhra. He was in Libya with us and he had this clairvoyance power to peep into the future.

"Is he still there or liberated", enquired another. "No, no not yet", replied the first man.

"What did he tell your wife?", the second Ghost was curious.

"He said she will have a happy married life with conjugal bliss embroidered all round and centre".

"Then how come you are here?", his listner wondered.

"Oh, the prediction was good for my wife only". She is having a good time with her present husband whom she married soon after my liberation by the lift shaft.

"How come?", queried the other.

It was a Friday. We were living in the fifth floor. Wife said that our overhead water tank is overflowing and I should rush to the basement to switch off the pump as the automatic system had failed.

"Then! Then what; 1 rushed through the open lift door at my floor there was but no lift".

"Where did the lift go".

It was under repair and was stranded between 5th and sixth floor.

The lift-man opened the lift door at fifth floor and had gone down to collect some tools through the other lift and he forgot to close the lift door of the second lift".

Oh, how sad, the other ghosts in the hearing sympathised with him.

"Not that sad for my wife who married my colleague who helped to get all compensation and Insurance money which comes to One Million rupees", concluded the ghost who was in Libya.

What we once thought as a blessing or gift and what we were eager to know from the Godmen is now a curse for us.

We are cursed to know everything which we now or ever wanted to know.

Oh, OH FORGIVE US LORD. spare us from this agony, oh Lord, we do not want to know, the muffled, noiseless, voiceless cries of hundred and thousand of ghost souls-rose in unison while the temple doors were opening, oh Lord, we Don't want to KNOW...

FOUR

The Bride and the Bugs

The Bride and the Bugs

"My boy will die of hunger; he did not have a drop of blood for the last four days", lamented the mother bug.

The bug family consisted of father bug, mother bug and two children, the eldest being a daughter. Till the other day they were living happily in a small pore in a wooden cot which had an occupier who left four days before.

"You are unnecessarily getting scared for nothing", said the father bug. "You know that we bugs can live without blood for months together. No doubt we will be paper thin and transparent by that time and will not be capable of moving around. We have to remain in our abode, hoping for a new dawn when a plum body may roll around and come near our homes, when we can have our bellies filled. Like the human beings, on whose blood we sustain, we also have to believe that tomorrow will be another day. And you are already over feeding the boy, he does not look like a baby bug but very much like a grown up bug", sermoned the father bug.

"You say things which I never or ever will understand", said the mother bug.

"That is because you are from the Gypsy lot", commented the father.

"What is this Gypsy lot father", mused the daughter bug.

"Look baby, like human being we also have classes and stratam. I belong to that class of bugs which believes in a home, well furnished, having balconies and lawns and we are happy in the home furniture and beds which men painstakingly accumulate in their life time.

"Your mother belongs to the Gypsy lot", continued the father, "Who have their homes in moving things like, state transport buses, trains and such other things which men have invented to carry them from place to place."

"What is wrong in that, tell me", the mother bug joined the issue with the father bug. "It is you who fell for me and not vice-versa", the mother bug was getting angry.

"How did that come about father", asked the daughter bug.

"I was happily passing my time in a Planter's guest house in Kerala. He had an assortment of girl friends who came with him to the guest house for short stays. One night after having my full bite I overslept in one of the discarded garment of one such girl and was carried away by her. When I woke up I was in one of the state transport buses going to Kovalam Beach. I slipped down and was looking for a place to hide. Then I met your mother who just then had her fill from an English lady tourist, and was going under the seat cover to join her family. I was so charmed by her glow because of the English blood filled in her", narrated the father bug.

"I always like English tourists. They all come in shorts irrespective of weather. Entry and exit are very easy with them. Even otherwise I hate the saree clad Indian ladies", commented the mother bug with contempt.

"Why mother , what is wrong with Indian ladies", asked the daughter. "Saree is a good cover for them. Nobody will know what they would be doing with the legs wrapped by the saree. When we attempt to crawl over their legs, they simply bring one leg against the other and crush us in between. This they will do without flincing an eye lid or show of any emotion. They will continue to do whatever they are doing without interruption like talking or reading or sewing.

"Yes, yes you are right mother", agreed the daughter. "It is difficult for those who are wearing jeans and long trousers to crush what is going up and down over their legs."

"Then what happened father", the daughter was eager to know.

"I ventured to enter your mother's family and asked for her wings which was reluctantly agreed to by your grandfather."

"Why?" asked the daughter.

"These gypsy lot normally do not like their women folk to go to static home" said the father.

"Then?" the daughter was anxious.

"However, I won over them and we moved to this house through the master of the house, when he boarded the bus on its return trip as his car broke down."

"Oh, those days were really good", reminiscised the mother bug.

"How?" asked the daughter.

We were in the master bedroom. The master of the house had an ongoing affair with the housemaid", said the father bug. "His wife was aware of it", interjected the mother bug.

"Yes, yes, she was", continued the father bug, whenever the master slipped into the maid's room, she would pretend to be asleep till he tip-toed back to the room. We would have our bite full and he would not move but would suffer the bite as she would be pretending to be asleep. When the master came to the bed, she would pretend to wake up and it would then be the Master's tum to pretend asleep. Then we would move to him for our further fill", explained the father bug.

All the bugs chuckled.

"Why the lady kept quite, I used to wonder", said the mother bug.

"Oh, she was saddist, she was knowing everything and was taking sweet revenge on both of them', said the father.

"How? " asked the mother.

"She used to mix some substance in the food of the master of the house and slowly he lost his senses and became a para-plegic. He is now fully bed ridden and the lady tortures him both physically and mentally", explained the father.

"And that housemaid", asked the daughter.

"Oh, the lady used to interchange the tablets which the master used to give the housemaid with identically looking vitamin tablets and that stupid maid conceived. The lady kept quite for the first few months, then shouted at the maid in full sight of the colony dwellers. Now| am told that she is begging at the entrance of the house with her child." concluded the father.

"Why did you move out of that room", asked the daughter.

"Alter the master was consigned to the store room, somehow I did not feel like remaining in that room. Moreover, the lady used to get restless and hardly slept in the night. I felt it an avoidable risk", said the father bug. "I felt that this guest room is safer, there is variety and the guests normally will not complain about bug bites as among human beings such complaints from the guests are deemed indescent", added the father.

"It is all OK, now tell me what we should do for the boy", the mother bug was impatient.

"See, the younger brother of the lady of the house is getting married today. The bride and the groom are expected by evening and when they retire to the bedroom we can send the boy there. " father bug had an answer.

"When there is a marriage in the house, there will be guests and some of them will be in this room too, so why should he be sent to the bedroom, why not he stay with us", reasoned the mother bug.

"Yes, guests will definitely come, but we do not know what type of people they are. There could be old ones, and it would be a tiresome job to travel through their wrinkled skin folds. Some of the guests may keep awake to play cards and crack lewd jokes. " Father bug placed his point of view.

"Will not the bride and groom also keep wake?" questioned the mother bug.

"Yes, keep awake they will, but-in the new found company and the associated euphorea they will hardly notice a bite here and there and even if they become aware of it they will take it as a mischief by the other. The last thing they expect are bugs in their bed." said the father.

"How will the boy reach there?" wondered the mother.

"Out the daughter can drop the boy at the window. From the window he can crawl to the head stead and he should move to the other end and slip down to the gap at the head joint which is a good shelter", the father detailed the modus-operandi.

"How can he go through the window, I remember you have said once that the windows and doors of newly wed human beings will be always tightly closed, in the night", the mother bug was suspicious.

"That they will be" said the father. "But you see tonight is a full moon night and these human beings have this funny notion that the face of their ladies resemble the full moon. To prove his point our stupid groom will also say the same thing and will point out the moon to his bride. It may even remain open for the whole night. And among them it is considered to indecent to peep into the bedroom or enter it even in the day light." The father explained his logic.

"I don't think so", said the mother bug, "that Astrologer Chandraji always goes to the bedroom first and he spends hours there on one pretext or the other to the utter discomfort of the couple", said the mother bug.

"No, what I said is of normal persons, Chandraji is a case of perversion and is an exception", said the father bug.

That night the boy bug was escorted by the sister upto the window. From there onwards the baby bug was on his own. It correctly moved from the window to the head stead of the bed and started crawling to the other end as explained by his father and reinforced by the mother many times thereafter.

The bride was angry. She was 29 plus. Everybody told, and she also knew that she was very ordinary, with no job, no accomplishments. Her sisters were smart, employed in multinationals and there were many fellow seeking their hand but none for her. At last, this fellow came with his sister to see her. They were greedy and the lady was vile. They bargained to the last penny with the father. Cash, jewellery, maruti car and what not: Her sisters and mother were grumbling that they have to shell out all their savings to see her off with a "Mangal Sutra." She was angry and mentally agitated and as she normally did on such occasions she started fiddling with the bed-switch.

The bug had almost made it upto the other end of the head stead. Then the sudden flash of lights unnerved him. He jumped aimlessly.

The bride saw the bug falling. It lay motionless on the marble floor. A bug, a bug, the bride know them they were in her house too. They are wretched blood suckers. Like her sister-in-law and her own husband who sucked the last penny out of her poor father. She concentrated on the bug, and she felt that the bug lying before her is none but her new sister-in-law or her own husband, it made no difference, both were same. The bug remained motionless. The polished marble floor made it difficult to run fast towards the bed stand. And then the light which was flashing in and out, the bug was in total confusion.

The bride knew that her husband had come to the room, he had changed to some night dress and was saying something to her. She did not hear, nor did she want to hear. She tensed, pressed the heel to the floor, crooked the right foot toe and paced it firmly upon the bug and slowly drew an arc. She felt relieved and an unknown calm enveloped her. She could now hear her husband. "I know, I know", he was saying. You are shy to admit it. I was asking you, am I not handsome. Instead of saying it by words, you drew a half circle with your toe. That is what the Indian women normally do when they want to express their admiration for their husband, but are shy of telling it. I do not know how many circles you are going to draw to night, HA, HA, HA, HO, HO!

FIVE
BHAVAYAMI

Bhavayami

In the head lights of the car Unni saw his father standing beneath the tamarind tree. The track leading to his house branched off from the main street from there. From the tree it was another two hundred yards to his house. It was Unni's ancestral house, a huge house in the midst of coconut trees, mango trees, jack fruit trees and so on. The tamarind tree was close to the entrance from where the track began. The servant closed the main gate once UNNI returned from the town where he had his Architectural firm. His father was in his usual white dhoti and an upper cloth tucked around his shoulder. His white beard and hair fluttered in the wild breeze. Unni stopped the car, switched off the headlights and walked upto his father. .

"You did not fear", said his father.

"No, Unni didn't fear", replied Unni.

When he was a boy of only six or seven his father used to jump behind him and make gunshot sounds to scare him and say "Unni is scared".

Unni would reply "Unni is not scared". This was their simple game.

"How are you there father?", asked Unni.

His father smiled, the same way when Unni used to ask "Where has mother gone?".

Unni's mother and her spinster sister were singers of some repute and when they were away on concerts, Unni would be alone with his father. His father was a scholar in Sanskrit and had some books to his credit. He belonged to a family of scholars and he, it is said, fell in love with Unni's mother when they met in a royal family wedding where she and her sister were giving a concert. Beauty and music were her forte and Unni's father felt both these qualities of her irresistable and inspite of protest from his family he married her. The discord started when she resumed singing in, public concerts when Unni was hardly a year old or so. Unni used to be left in the care of a distant aunt of hers and it was then that Unni's father realised that the family he hoped to raise was withering away. He withdrew unto himself to a world, where he, his books and Unni only mattered. Yet somehow they all remained as a family. Unni's father somehow was able to get back to his own home and spend more time with his brothers, sisters and uncles. He used to take Unni with him whenever he could and his wife did not object.

At his mother's place Unni found himself at times neglected. The house was always filled with music, swish of silk sarees, rush of cars bringing music club secretaries, stage contractors, mother and her sister hurrying out with flower decked hair, wrapped in silks accompanied by members of their troupe, all in a hurry and with little or no pause. It was that hurry which brought Unni closer to his father.

Rather than being head of a family, father reconciled himself to being a visitor in the family. Yet they still remained a family where people spoke not to be heard, looked not be seen, touched not to be felt. How strange it ought to be. Unni used to muse. To the utter discomfort of her sister Unni's mother gave birth to a daughter and withdrew herself from concert tours. For some time Unni's father felt that the family was again reshaping. But for Unni's mother the pull of fame, awards, good life and not the least the money and the comforts that came with them were stronger than the pull of the family While his sister remained under the total care of the old aunt, Unni's father ensured that his son was not distanced from him. He put Unni in a school near his House and after the school Unni was sent to Bangalore for higher studies and was put in the hostel. It was curious, Unni used to think, all in the three corners for a triangle. Time tamed everyone, the concerts became fewer in number, Unni's mother used to visit him at the hostel, Unni visited his sister and mother at their place, father visited Unni at the hostel, all visitors at each others' place. An endless musical chair, it was:

"I know what you are thinking, forget it Unni, those are memories we hope to forget but dread forgetting."

"Are you happy there father?", Unni repeated his question.

"I am above the state of happiness Unni. What is there to be happy and unhappy. Life everywhere has a pattern, the helplessness of the infancy, the autocracy of the parents, the push to run ahead of others, a life on which you hardly have any say, everything is thought and decided by the parents, what to eat, to drink, to dress, and then the race to get a foothold in life, then the struggle to climb, reach the top, to have a spouse,. set up a home, harmony in between distrust, fear of walkover & adultery, children, the wheel turns full, again back to insecurity and helplessness of infancy at old age. Tell me is there anything different. Yet when we pass through any of these phases we feel they are especially for us and whatever was accomplished we only could, and none else. It is all a wild goose chase, a big wild goose chase, that was life Unni, that was life...... I am sorry Unni. this etemal thirst is driving me mad, otherwise I would not have troubled you by standing here, I knew it is not fair and expected. Once gone from here we are there and you are here. The demarcation is clear, we go with what we have eared and leave our place for you to earn what we could not. I am not speaking about material wealth we painstakingly accumulate, it is something else which you will not understand now. I have left the stage for you and once bowed out of it none could come back to mend what he erred".

"I remember you always father', Unni almost in tears.

"Yes you will, for some more time. Then I will give way for other stronger memories. It is the natural order and there is no exception.

"I don't think so", Unni tried to protest.

"It has to be like that only, Unni, like that only, every first child brings an excitement to the parents, he or she is an anticipated intruder, a guest awaited. making the duo a trio. A meaning is inferred to every noise, a smile, a cry and the whole world of parents zeroes in on the happiness or unhappiness of that tiny tot. That tiny tot slowly grows to a world governed by sanctions. love linked to good behaviour, conditional and the alienation process sets in. The child learns that compliance to parental code alone shall bring his needs to fulfillment. Many submit to it and a few revolt and become what is loosely termed as 'drop outs'. The transition from a child to a son and daughter and from father to 'The father' is an uncomprehendably long process. By the time the father Starts to look upon the son for support and company, the father becomes. the proverbial 'Old man' and an object of ridicule. This is a universal process, nothing special for you or for me. I had-forgotten my father, so shall you too. It is the order.

"No, you were always different", said Unni.

"Oh, that is another false notion. Every father will feel that his son or daughter is very special, the children will think their parents are special, then nobody is special. All are just ordinary, that's it, just ordinaries. How many special sons burn the special daughters of others in the confinement of their special rooms, Is it not Unni?", Unni shuddered. The sight of the half charred body of his sister flashed off. He wanted to shake off that sordid sight from his memory. "You cannot Unni, you cannot, if, by shaking the 'head you can shake of memories, you will hardly find any still head in this world".

"You are sarcastic as ever", said Unni.

"It is how you look at it, I am what I am".

That was it, thought Unni, he was what he was, living in a family who were all strangers to each other, where they would listen but not hear, Speak but not be spoken to, touch but not feel, curious it was.

"The thirst, you mentioned, what is that?" asked Unni. .

"Oh! I cannot explain it. Not only me but many among us suffer by that eternal thirst, it is drying us up. That is why I thought I must meet you, many among us try to meet those we have left behind, but only few, it seems among us are bestowed with that privilege.

"What can I do for that? I will do whatever you ask for. Just tell me", Unni was earnest.

"Just tell, that is it, seek, you shall be given, isn't it so Unni. When you were a child I knew what you needed- may be a new pen, an umbrella, a watch, may be a new shirt... no father needs to be told what his child needs, they knew it, in the eyes of the children. But all pretend that they don't know it. You should ask so that you could be reminded of the parental code of compliance", His father laughed.

"I seek no compliance from you", said Unni.

"You cannot Unni, I am beyond compliances, none of your writ shall run on me".

"Please father, please stop it", Unni was in tears.

"Nothing much Unni, nothing much. just let water onto parched fields, allow water to a. thirsty throat, be it animal or human, don't drive them away, the water you let to a parched land, to a dry throat, a pittance given to a needy, all that quenches our thirst and brings us relief. In today's world when everyone is on the run after mirages, who has time to stop and listen to a muffled cry, a wailing heart, time to put a bowl of water to the cupped hands. But if you can do that, that is our relief from this damned thirst and not by the rice balls you offer once a year on a river side topped by sesame. Never that Unni, never, we are above hunger of rice balls, seasames.

"I shall father, I will". Unni felt a new firmness in his own voice.

"OK Unni, I must leave now, it is getting late for you, Sumitra will be worried. Sumitra was Unni's wife.

"Just one thing father", Unni hesitated.

"Whats that? asked his father.

"Is mother around you", asked Unni.

"We don't see as you think, but I am sure she is always around me I can feel her".

"How is she?", Unni could not help asking.

"She ought to be at peace, she pursued a course which she felt right and proper for her. As usual I could not see the way she looked at the whole matter". His father sounded melencholic.

The lined up bodies, fished out from the water filled quarry where the music party's car dived down, down the deep. water. Unni was at Bangalore; he reached in time to lit the two pyres. He again began shaking his head.

"Don't worry, she is in peace, she taught me what she could not when she was alive that there is nothing as right and wrong. It is the way we look at them. I hoped to chain her to me, for which I had no right. Then what you have been doing to Sumitra is not right, whatever way you look at it". His father was passive.

"No, I did not', Unni attempted to protest, but his voice was feeble.

"Look Unni, his father said in a solemn sound, a marriage is a holy sacrement a union of two human beings that is destined. It is witnessed by all the sacred elements of this Universe and we bygones look for the dawn of a new generation. There is no justification for being unfaithful to one's spouse. You feel that Sumitra is not a modern woman of your city concept. She may not be. But there are a hundred things where she is ahead of you. By shortening the hair and keeping ferocious dogs in the home, no wife becomes modern overnight. She is light years ahead of you in her total devotion to you and the family you are raising. You are forgetting that the clandestine affair you are nursing with your colleague's wife will bring upon you, her and her husband and above all on, Sumitra and your son, nothing but calamity and sorrow. Watch my word, nothing but calamity and sorrow. You may not know why some of us are still wandering around. It is the load of our sins that are weighing us down stopping us from crossing over to the world where we ought to be. Our sins are like boulders on our head, the load is transferred when you commit a similar sin. Then our load is shifted and kept ready to be put on your head when you arrive. Mercifully enough I did not have much load, except perhaps suspecting your mother, yet your clandestine affairs will take away that load too, but frankly I don't want that, I would love to carry the load eternally rather than pass on to you. You are the one I ever deeply loved and | don't want you to be the load bearer for my sins. Now my time is up Unni, I must go".

"I must go", that is what he used to tell, after the mother perished in the accident, followed by the burning of his sister at her husband's house. And he went. .

"Please don't go, please", Unni iried to grab where he thought his father was standing.

"What are you doing here?", It was Sumitra. "I had seen the Car taking the turn but you stopped in between. What happened?

"He was here", I spoke to him', said Unni.

"Who", asked Sumitra.

"Father, who else, he said he is thirsty", Unni was sobbing.

"I know it is hard, but we have to accept the realities as they come before us. It is almost one year isn't it?"

Unni looked at the charred parch of the land behind the tamarind tree. It is where they cremated him. It is where they found him dead. The hibiscus have flowers.

"Yes, I understand that he is not here. He had gone, it may be my illusion, yet I felt it so real. Dead cannot come back. They are gone for ever. Gone for ever", Unni sighed.

"No, they are not gone, said Sumitra, look at our son, does he not have the same gait of your father, the nose, the way he rubs his chin, he is there in you and through you in our son. Then may be to his son and so on. Something will be always there reminding us of those we think had gone. Death can only take away but it cannot wipe away. They shall live in our memories and they leave mark on their progenies. Leave the car here. We will walk the remaining way. I feel so close to you, so close, let us not talk but walk, through the path, through the fields may be to the end of this earth, till we are tired and slip down hand in hand, holding each other", Sumitra said like reciting a poem.

From the sudden stillness, Unni heard the crooning of the violin, the humming of a Thambura, tappings on the Mridangam, and the air filled with the fragrance of jasmine in bloom, and he could hear his mother singing "BHAVAYAMI..."

He closed his eyes, drew Sumitra close to him, held her tight as if to hold those precious moments for ever from slipping.

SIX
GOD'S SMILE

God's Smile

"Poor mother, she cried a lot begging to let her go, but of what use, the slowly and slowly sawed her neck off", said the young hen sobbing.

"It is our-fate and destiny my little one", said the elder hen of the two. "We are destined to be cut and sliced and fried to be eaten by our masters who had paid for us. Some cut our head in one slash and some slowly saw us as warranted by their religion".

"Why so, why not in the reverse that we cut and slice them so they also knew how it will be", said the younger hen in anger.

"No, it cannot be like that my children", said the senior cock who was listening "That is not in the natural order".

"We don't want to know what that order is, whatever be that order we lost our mother today and few days back our father too", said the younger one in all bitterness.

They were in the backyard of the residential quarters of a construction company. The staff occupying these quarters used to buy hens, cocks & chick which were collectively called as 'Chicken' by them. The two small hens were in fact not from the broiler lot, where they come out of a machine called incubator. They came to this world in an accepted natural way by the union of a male and a female. Their parents were supplied to one of the staff members by a local in return for favours received by way of a stepiny tyre given by him when the focal was found stranded in a forlorn stretch of a road somewhere in the desert. Then this staff member got abruptly transferred to a far away place when the company found out that De used to barter not only stepiny tyres but other costlier items too in rectum of many consumables. His move was so instant that he did not get enough time to appropriately enjoy his supply. Knowing his miserly ways his friends also did not attempt to appropriate the chickens for themselves. His miserly ways included squeezing the last particle of tooth-paste from the tube with the help of a roller pin besides using the soap till it ultimately dissolves on his body without leaving any trace of its original existence in any shape or form.

Consequently, the hen and cock were left alone and as they needed no Paraphemalia, that goes with the union of a man & woman they floated and mated as freely and frequently as they could and a long chain of chics followed which were promptly eaten by the wild cats and dogs that were also abundant in the camp area. In between, the aforesaid employee came for a one night halt in the camp which brought an untimely end to the father cock. Among the number of chics that came out of her eggs these two small hens survived, mysterious: though it is. The helpless widow found herself in an unenviable position when she had to ward off the attacks on her children by dogs and cats besides feeding them.

Then the senior cock came to the scene. "He was an owner less cock without any particular abode to claim for. Being a loner he perfected his skills of survival by skilfully dodging the attempt of workers of the camp to cook him. Later finding such chases a waste of time the workers left him to his fate, which was not immediately to end up in their frying pans. He took upon himself the protection of the children and the mother hen. She however, was not in a mood to go for more chics knowing the futility of momentory pleasures attained in ridiculous postures to bring them in when they have to ultimately end up on the dining tables. The senior cock was in thick friendship with a grand cock living with his family in another camp nearby.

This grand cock had a lot of clairvoyance power and could peep into the future of other hens and cocks. And they flooded him always to find out how best they could postpone their final liquidation, which is any way imminent, by a few more days or for atleast some hours. The grand cock peeped into their future and came with many remedies and suggestions and one such remedy was to eat some special stones with their grains. Notwithstanding his wisdom and clairvoyance powers the grand cock cannot contain his excitement when he had to deal with young hens and chics. For a closer scrutiny of their fate he would bring them under his wings and if his wife was not watching, would give some quick rubs on their sensitive parts. The young hens never bothered to complain as the experience was not altogether bad and what was the point in protesting when their eventual termination at the dining tables were only a few days or hours away. The husband cocks also pretended that they were not watching the grand cock was believed to hold the key to peep into their future, and moreover, the grand cock never advanced beyond a few rubbings as his old age prevented him from anything further.

From the association of the grand cock the senior cock learnt a lot about divinity, natural order so forth an so on and by meditating by himself he felt that he could find answers to many questions of which the grand cock was either not aware or not bothered to ponder about.

" I will tell you of the natural order and how our destinies are interwoven with it", said the senior cock.

"May I join you sir, said a small white dog which came limping towards them, What happened", asked the senior cock.

"My father broke my forearm, I am in great pain", weeped the little dog.

"Why? asked the young hen.

"See little girl", said the senior cock. "The soul in this little dog is of the son of the officer who fives there in the family accommodation. His son died about an year ago when bitten by a dog affected by rabbies. Because it was a case of liberation of soul before time, the boy's soul tried to get in to their household back through his mother. But since she had implanted some device made of copper he could not get through her in the previous household. As his time was running out he allowed his soul to pass through the dog family of the neighbouring officer. He was so fond of his younger sister, so, whenever he could get time he used to ran to his human family to play with his sister. His human father who already lost a son by dog bite would not allow any more dogs to enter in the family. Today he broke his arms. "Is that not so?" questioned the senior cock. "Yes sir", said the little dog weeping.

"Don't weep after all the poor man did not know that you are none but his dead son. It is their curse my boy, not knowing that the dog they stone away, the bird they catapult, the cat they run over, the lamb they slice all have the soul of their lost ones, who were trying perhaps to have glimpse of them.", the senior cock assuaged the little dog.

"I don't know sir, why God has been so cruel to me. I had a comfortable home, a loving mother, a cute sister and above all a caring father. And in one dog bite I lost everything. And see my father who nurtured and pampered me and gave me all the love he could, today broke my arms and left me limping.

"Don't try to bring God in between you and your father", said the senior cock. "Like the human being who eats and beat us you also do not know what the God is".

"Then, what is God, sir, asked the little dog. Ah, tell us who is the God, my mother also cried today calling for the God when the cook was sawing off her neck this morning", said the elder hen.

"OK, I will tell you who and what God is, listen carefully", said the senior cock. They listened. Along with them the wind listened, the leaves listened, the clouds above them listened, all diving and non living objects around them listened.

"GOD, started the senior cock, is everything in this world. Not only in the world we live but also in the hundreds of galaxies ever explored by man and in millions of stars yet to be explored by him. He is the universe which encompasses every object both tangible and intangible and abstract and non-abstract. As the stupid men say he is not everywhere but he is the everything. He.is the leaves and also the branch holding the leaves and the very earth holding the tree. He is the air we breathe, the water we drink, the food we take and the waste our bodies discharge. He is the flower and the worm too. His perception is according to one's imagination. He is either doing any good for you-as he is not doing any bad for you. He is not giving anyone a good time or a bad time. It is we who make our good and bad time. What is good for the thief is never good for the thieved. What one experiences as good-or bad is according to his choice. What is good and bad is a relative concept. 6 is nothing as universally good or bad. It is how we look at them. God is the temple and the variety of idols man make, he is the book they read and the book they worship like he is the temple, he is their toilet too. If the man wants to see God he can see and feel him in his toilet also. It is all in one's mind. He has no day and dawns. He has no time. He neither travels backwards nor forward. Time is a human concept and not of God. It is we who travel to, him, travel through him and travel beyond him. He doesn't age, it is we living organism that age. Time has no relevance to God, it is a human concept to correlate their mundane activities in the world, with which God has no concern. He is the victor and vanquished. He is the butcher, his knife and the little lamb that is sliced by the knife. He is the snake and the snake charmer. He is the light and the darkness. In excitement, the senior cock gasped for air"

"I don't know why you have to say all these things, after all you are only a cock, the writer should have given this duty to some of his fellow human beings", said the cat who too was listening.

"Yes, but he says he has a problem that if he takes any name and bring a human being as a character he would be made to apologise both standing and stooping", said the senior cock. "Why?", asked the cat. "Because while human population is around 6 billion the names to identify them from one another are still only in millions. So naturally on an average there may be one million people with the same name. Thus when a name figures in a story somebody somewhere will identify himself with the character of the story and shall ask for the head of the writer. So no names. Moreover, the writer is busy writing an article captioned "A comparative study of bottom girth of yesteryear Hindi film heroines with todays heroines", an article which he feels that His Majesty would approve for publication, unlike the one he disapproved on 'Ghosts and Bugs'. Let me continue, explained the senior cock.

"So when there is no difference between the killer and the killed and all is part of the same right down to the last atom why cry my little hen over your slaughtered mother. After some time it may be your turn. But why worry, once you knew that, the knife that will slaughter you, the cook, the frying pan all is none but God himself like you, Where is the wound, where is the pain, oh my little hen. !f anyone thinks that he inflicts pain on another it is foolhardy, because he is inflicting pain on himself. Once this realisation dawns that all is one and one is all there is no jubiliation on victory nor depression on defeat. Everything is same, nothing good or bad, neither sick nor healthy, no loss or gain, everything is one and all and same, Oh God, forgive us", concluded the senior cock.

"If it is so why these human beings divide themselves among so many religions and kill each other", querried the cat.

1 cannot say, replied the senior cock, must be by ignorance, from time immemorial man invented religion, worships, rituals all in an attempt to hold the unholdable, to fathom, the unfathomable, a pursuit for their own peace to find the ultimate truth which is nothing but he himself".

Suddenly a chill shriek rose in the stillness. "Oh, it is the grand cock", said the senior cock. 'His masters have come from Canada, he is being readied for the dinner which they always take late".

"How come that the grand cock did not knew that he will end up on their dinner plate today when he predicts for everyone else", wondered the little dog.

'That is the trouble my boy", explained the senior cock. 'While one can see back of the other he can not see it for himself similarly, they can predicts for others but not for themselves, the same happened with the grand cock too. Let us pray that he become a good dish for his masters. It is getting cold, come my little hens I| will hold you under my wings, he said, I will take a small nap before I announce the arrival of the dawn through my clarion call".

"Why should you announce the dawn through your clarion call for these heartless human beings, said the irritated younger hen, let there be no dawn".

"Oh, my silly child it is my duty in this world to announce the dawn. Not only me, thousands of other cock join me to announce the arrival of the dawn. Dawn will be there even if I don't give the clarion call. But if I don't give my call I will be failing in my destined duty. I cannot do that, come what may, I will give my call even if I have to apologise for it sooner or later. Come under my wings', said the senior cock.

The hens moved, the listening wind moved, the leaves moved, the heavens flashed the thunder, the clouds let loose the rains, a torrential rain followed.

Mrs. Rajendran woke up when the sudden cool wind entered through their bedroom window. Rain drops slashed along with the wind. She rose from the bed and moved towards the window to close it. She found the senior cock holding the two hens under the sun shade. She called Rajendran who was still curled up and in an inebriated state after his usual fill of drinks.

"See here one old cock is holding two hens under him and while you cannot hold even one under you", she giggled mischieviously. In the state he was, the God in his lips smiled...